10/5/06

To lovely Sadie,

A more beautiful butterfly has never been; your flight is our privilege to observe.

Upon my return from Cape May, love, Mom.

When the Monarchs Fly

by Robert J. Myers

illustrated by Cricket McGehee

Harvey Cedars, New Jersey

Down The Shore Publishing Corp.
Box 3100, Harvey Cedars, NJ 08008

www.down-the-shore.com

The words "Down The Shore" and its logos are registered U.S. Trademarks.

Manufactured in Canada
10 9 8 7 6 5 4 3 2 1
First printing, 2001.

Cover illustration by Cricket McGehee
Book design by Leslee Ganss.

Library of Congress Cataloging-in-Publication Data

Myers, Robert J. 1934-
    When the monarchs fly / by Robert J. Myers ; illustrated by Cricket McGehee.
        p. cm.
    Summary: A young girl worries that she will be separated from her home and neighbors, just like the injured butterfly stranded in the backyard of her Cape May, New Jersey, home. Includes facts about the Monarch butterfly.
    ISBN 0-945582-76-5 (cloth)
    [1. Moving, Household--Fiction. 2. Monarch butterfly--Fiction. 3. Butterflies--Fiction. 4. Cape May (N.J.)--Fiction.]   I. McGehee, Cricket, ill. II. Title.
  PZ7.M9914 Wh 2001
  [Fic]--dc21

                                    2001037114

For Joyce
who gave me Cape May

contents

When the Monarchs Fly

Autumn

O f all the seasons of the year, Ellie would miss early Autumn the most. For that was when all the winged creatures came through Cape May on their long flight south. There were the seabirds who crowded the shorelines to eat their fill of small crabs, fattening and strengthening themselves to fly to Central or South America. There were high-flying hawks who brought a sense of sky-dazzle, of sky-danger. There were the neon blue and green dragonflies, zigging and zagging through the pretty yards of the old seaside resort. Old timers called them the devil's sewing needles and said that if you weren't careful, they'd sew your mouth shut. But, most pleasing of all to Ellie, were the Monarch butterflies. She thought they were the prettiest, the gentlest of all the migrators. In early September the first of them could be seen, bringing in their train thousands and thousands more, like a loose cloud stretching out over hundreds of miles. Their wings were a strong bright orange, sharply divided by curving strokes of black. People said that they looked like the stained glass windows in a church. But Ellie thought that that wasn't right. Stained glass windows were too still, there was no movement to them.

To Ellie, everything about the Monarchs spoke of movement. She loved their crazy flight, that slow, graceful, jerky path they took through the air. They were like leaves falling, falling and catching themselves, rising and then falling again. It was as if they lived in a world where there were no straight lines. Only swoop and fall and glide and rise. When a Monarch flew through her own backyard, Ellie would run beside it and pretend she was one of them. She flapped her arms and she rose on tiptoe, then suddenly she would fall low, almost to her knees, twisting and duck-walking till she rose again with a happy cry. Often she got so dizzy she fell to the ground laughing.

In the few weeks that they sheltered in and around Cape May, the Monarchs clustered on

When the Monarchs Fly

the bushes and small trees. They were so thick that the bushes seemed to have changed color; their wings fluttered and the bushes seemed on fire. Then, when their time in Cape May was up, these frail creatures would head out over Delaware Bay toward their destination far to the south. To Ellie they seemed so brave. To go on that journey of a thousand miles, over sea and mountain and swamp and city!

Ellie, though, didn't want to leave Cape May. This was the only home she had ever known. The small two-story house, painted gaily in beige and dusty rose and lavender like the large old Victorian homes that made the town famous, was the only house she had ever lived in. And her neighborhood, of houses different from hers but nearly the same size, some single and some attached, but all so familiar, just like the people who lived in them, like old Mrs. Greer and the Dunlaps, the Cranes and Fortinos. This was her neighborhood and she loved it. So when one day, playing outside by herself near the kitchen window, she overheard her parents talking between themselves about her father traveling up the coast to North Jersey or south to Delaware to find work, she grew frightened.

Her father ran a party fishing boat for Mr. Jackson; it was one of the two boats that Mr. Jackson owned and her parents' talk had to do with that.

"I don't care if it's his boat," she heard her father say angrily to her mother. "I was there for eight years before that nephew of his came along. If anyone should get a crack at buying it, it's me."

"But, Larry," her mother had answered, "people like to keep businesses in the family. It's his nephew. He has the right to sell the boat to whoever he wants. And you can get a job with another boat...."

"Oh no! Every boat in the marina has a captain and I'm not going to be first mate again on anybody's boat. Not after they all know why I'm not heading the Lady Cape any more."

"But captain jobs open up, too...remember the one last year...."

He didn't want to hear any more.

They never spoke to her directly about it, were not aware that she knew anything about it, but she could tell that it was on their minds. Whenever she entered the room and they stopped talking, she knew they had been talking about that. Whenever she saw a large cardboard box in the house, even the box holding their new television, she wanted to rip it into pieces, afraid that the packing had already started.

When the Monarchs Fly

13

The Monarch

This year the Monarchs came and went. Ellie's father, as he did each year, had taken her out to the nature walk at Cape May Point to see them. The butterflies could gather here on the edge of the ocean in great numbers. So many fluttered about that some even landed on her, their long skinny legs as light as snowflakes on her head.

"Quick, daddy, I'm like a bush! Take my picture!" she shouted.

He took a snapshot of her that came out perfectly—the small brown-haired girl with a two-butterfly crown.

In the third week of October, long after it seemed all the Monarchs had flown away, Ellie was surprised to see the familiar loopy flight of orange and black in her backyard. She stared out the kitchen window at the slowpoke.

"Hey!" she called out, "don't you know you shouldn't be here?"

She ran outside. There had been time for the Monarch to leave the yard, but it was still there. It had settled on a leaf of the crepe myrtle tree. For a moment, Ellie stood back, not wanting to frighten it.

"You better get going," she said. "You got a long flight and maybe somebody's waiting for you."

The butterfly slowly raised
and lowered its wings. Ellie thought that it really
looked like it was listening.

"It was cold last night," she said. "There was
even frost on the grass this morning. You get
frost on your wings and you're going to be in

real trouble. So you just fly out of here. Right now. I mean it. You get going."

The wings rippled in the breeze. Ellie stepped closer. She took another step, expecting the butterfly to leap into the air. But it didn't. She put her face right up to it.

She was so close she could see the jet black antennae and the short, fine black hairs on its body.

She walked around the butterfly and gently shook the tree limb. The butterfly rode up and down on the swaying branch.

"Don't you have any sense at all?" She put her face right up to the butterfly's, as if there would be an expression there to tell her what to say.

Then she saw something that made her heart stop. At the top of the wings were several small rips. The wings were no longer whole but were almost in separate pieces.

At that moment a small open-bed truck pulled into the drive. Ellie heard her father call out to her.

"Hey there, kiddo, what're you doing?"

She ran to him and told him about the butterfly. She held his hand and pulled him to the crepe myrtle tree.

"See? See him?"

Her father hands were rough and split from salt water and the sharp ends of a thousand hooks but he still could hold things lightly and surely. He lifted the leaf from below till it was almost at his eye level.

"I see," he said. "The poor little thing."

"What are we going to do for him?" Ellie asked.

"I'm not sure what we can do, Ellie."

"Can we take him inside and make him better?"

"I don't think you can treat butterflies,

honey. They're not like dogs or sick birds...."

"But why? He's sick, there must be something to make him better...."

Her father let the leaf return to its normal position.

"We don't know a lot about things like migrating, Ellie...all we know is that sometimes they have to move from one place to another...like people do...."

"People don't have to move," Ellie said.

He stared at her for a moment and seemed about to say something, then changed his mind and said, "Well, butterflies do...so maybe he's not as bad as he looks and if we leave him to himself, he'll rest for a while and then go on his way...."

"Do you think so?"

He shrugged his shoulders and tried to look hopeful.

"There's not much else we can do...."

Left Behind

Inside the house, Ellie helped her mother cook and set the table. But her mind was on the butterfly and she kept running to the window to look out. It was as if the whole world was dimming and the only bright spot in it was that small patch of orange.

Soon darkness covered even the spot of orange. Only the lights from the neighbors' houses could be seen through the trees.

At dinner, Ellie barely ate. Her parents could only look at one another, wanting to say something to her to ease her mind.

"Darling," her mother, who looked like Ellie but with all the features more defined and larger, finally said, "we'd like to help...but it's only a butterfly and you're going to make yourself sick dwelling on it like this...."

"I'll tell you what," her father said. "We'll wait an hour, give it a chance to get going, then we'll take a flashlight out to see it, okay?"

That was better than sitting inside, so Ellie said, "Okay."

After looking at her schoolbooks for an hour, her father switched on his strong-beamed flashlight and the three of them followed its light into the long yard, which was surrounded by sweetgum trees and white pines.

"It was right on the branch over here," said Ellie. "Shine the light here."

The brilliant orange seemed to leap out of the darkness.

"Oh I'm sorry, darling," her mother said and held her by the shoulder.

"Let him be then, Ellie." Her father stopped her from reaching out. "It could be he's just sleeping, getting his strength back. In the morning, he'll fly off...wait and see."

Ellie looked at the Monarch. It didn't seem to have moved at all. Maybe it really was sleeping.

The night seemed endless to Ellie. But when the first pale gray ocean-light brightened her room, she was out of bed.

Hurriedly she dressed and ran to the backyard in her bare feet. Even from the door she could see the Monarch still on the tree.

A thin coating of silvery frost covered the leaves. A crystal of ice seemed to flash on its wings.

"Wake up, please...wake up, butterfly!"

She raised and lowered the branch. When it didn't move, she gently touched its soft wing with her finger. There was no response. A little flap of wing formed by the two rips hung limply. She put her finger under its legs, hoping so strongly that it would crawl onto her. "Please...please...," she whispered.

"Ellie!" came her mother's voice from behind her.

She turned around, her eyes brimming. "Mommy...I think he's dead...."

Her mother touched the butterfly with the nail of her finger. She prodded the black body.

"I think so, too, darling. Oh dear...come on back inside now, there's nothing you can do for it."

Ellie's tears flowed freely. Her mother brushed the damp hair out of Ellie's eyes.

"Darling, it's a butterfly...."

"But they're waiting...!" Her small body shook with her sobs.

"Larry," her mother said to her father who was coming from the house, "say something to her. The butterfly's dead...."

"I was afraid of that," he said. "Listen, Ellie sweetheart...."

He took the slim girl into his arms and held her and gently rocked her until her sobbing stopped.

"Ellie...," he said, "Ellie...do you think we should bury him in the back yard?"

He could feel her head, pressed against his neck, shaking no.

"What then? You don't want to just leave him on the tree, do you?"

Again he felt the movement of her head telling him that she didn't want that either.

He picked her up and looked into her red eyes.

"Do you have something else in mind?"

This time she nodded yes. He waited a moment while she rubbed the back of her hand across her eyes. Her voice was faint when she finally spoke.

"I want to put him in the bay," she said.

"Just that, put him in the bay?"

She nodded, then added, "On a raft...so that it sails out into the bay...."

"Well...I think we can do that. Don't you think we can, Shar?"

His wife stroked Ellie's fine hair. "We'll build a nice raft, darling, a really nice raft."

The Raft

So Ellie's father nailed together a few small pieces of wood from an old shingle that was in the storage shed; he made an 8-inch raft, strong enough to float high on the waves of Delaware Bay.

Ellie broke off the long oval leaf that the butterfly was on. The Monarch was still standing; there was no way to tell that he was dead, except for the fact that he didn't move. Ellie, with great care, placed the leaf in the center of the raft.

In her father's truck, the three of them drove out to Higbee Beach. Ellie was in the middle, the butterfly-raft in her lap. The eyes of her parents glanced down to the butterfly every now and then but no one spoke.

The beach was empty of people. A few gulls flew high overhead, their cries thin and sharp, and sandpipers darted along the surf line. The bay was calm that day and a thin haze of cloud covered the sky. The water in close was a dull greenish color and toward the horizon it grew bluish gray and blended with the sky so that there was no clear separation between sky and bay.

"We're in luck," her father said. "Looks like the tide's been going out for an hour or so. And the waves aren't very high...the raft should sail pretty good."

"Go on, honey, put the butterfly in the water now," her mother said.

Ellie held the raft gently and, still in her bare feet, walked a few steps into the surf. Her mother and father took a few steps backwards. She lowered her hands to the water, letting them dip under the surface so that the raft broke free

When the Monarchs Fly

of her and bobbed easily on top. She straightened it for the butterfly to look straight out across the water. Then she bent over and whispered to it.

"Goodbye, sweet Monarch. Thank you for coming into our back yard and letting me see you. I wish you had flown away by yourself and caught up with all your family and friends. But if one of them is coming back for you, then he'll see you on the way to Mexico."

The raft slowly started to move away from her, as if being tugged at by invisible fingers. Ellie reached out and laid a finger ever so softly against the rips in the beautiful wing. The unseen tide drew the raft away and she watched the orange patch get smaller and smaller.

Lost

Her parents hoped that would be the end of the butterfly and that Ellie's sadness would disappear. But each day they saw that she was moping about, listless and daydreamy in a sad way. She barely smiled and could often be found in the backyard near the crepe myrtle tree.

She also walked around the neighborhood,

doing things like counting the houses and counting the crooked sycamore trees that grew along the curbs. It was as if by doing this she could stay longer.

"They payin' you to count those trees?" called down Mr. Fortino from his porch. He was her best friend Regina's grandfather.

Ellie blushed to be caught like this; she was actually pointing to each tree as she counted, and her hand was still in the air.

"Just kiddin'," he said with a laugh. "You want to see Regina? She's just inside doin' some homework."

She couldn't bring herself to answer him. Funny, though, to see him standing on the porch, a short man, always in old, old working clothes without a shape to them, his left leg bent at the knee from a long-ago accident. He was like the lumpy, knotted trees, she thought, and the thought almost took her breath away.

At dinner that night while Ellie silently picked at her food, her mother said to her, "Darling, you're not still thinking about that butterfly, are you?"

Ellie spoke with her face down. Her voice was so shaky that her parents hesitated before saying more.

"He must have moved way out in the ocean now and I don't know if the other butterflies found him at all...and he's so lonely...."

Her mother laid her hand over Ellie's hand. The larger hand was sweaty while Ellie's was as cold as ice. The eyes of her parents met painfully.

"Is that what you're worried about, that he won't be found?" her mother asked.

Ellie nodded up and down.

"But, darling...." Her mother sighed and seemed to search for the right words. "Darling, you saw all the butterflies that came through Cape May...there were millions...."

She caught her husband's eye; he was telling her not to continue that line of thought.

"Let the butterfly, go, baby, just let him go...." Then Ellie's mother suddenly changed the tone of her voice. "Next week is Halloween! Have you forgotten? And we haven't even talked about your costume...."

"I know!" her father said. "Why don't you go out as captain of a fishing boat. Just like your old man. You can wear my cap and I'll give you a net and a gaff! What do you think of that?"

The words that were meant to cheer her seemed to take something from her.

"May I leave the table," she said.

When they didn't answer, she pushed her chair back and ran from the room.

The Costume

The next day her father asked her if she had decided to go out on Halloween as a fishing boat captain.

"I don't think I want to do that," she said.

"Why?"

"Nobody wants them."

"What do you mean, Ellie? Everybody wants a captain."

She put her head down and didn't answer him.

"Ellie...who doesn't want a captain?"

"...Mr. Jackson...."

"Where did you hear that?"

She looked up at him, looking straight at him but with eyes full of uncertainty. This time he didn't press for an answer.

Later, her mother offered to take her to the variety store on the downtown mall to choose any costume she wanted. But nothing interested her.

"Ellie, we've looked at every costume in town and you haven't liked any of them. You don't think it's going to fall from the sky, do you?"

Ellie spoke almost to herself, "I'll make my own then."

Each night after dinner she went straight to her room and stayed there till bedtime. Though she was quiet her parents could hear her moving about. They were growing more frustrated trying to get her to talk with them.

"Did you tell her about leaving?" her

When the Monarchs Fly

father finally asked his wife.

"Me? Why would I say anything? Why are you asking?"

"Ellie knows."

"But how?"

"I don't know...all I know is that she knows and she's holding it inside."

On the night before Halloween, with the door closed, she went to

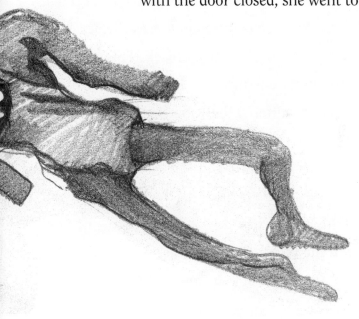

her closet and reaching into the very back, behind the clothes and games, took out a large paper bag. From it she pulled out her black body-suit and laid it on the bed. She reached in again and removed two large pieces of thin cardboard; they were unevenly shaped, torn from the flaps of a large box. These she placed one on each side of the body-suit. They were bright orange, as bright as her watercolors could make them. And the orange was divided into sections by lines of deep black. This was her Halloween costume. It looked like a huge Monarch butterfly, but one that had no head, one whose empty form had no life to it.

Without trying it on, she folded the costume and returned it to the bag. Halloween night would be the right time to put the costume on for the first time.

That night she dreamt that she was out at

sea and a storm was rising. The waves were enormous and she felt herself being lifted high, then dropping so fast that her stomach ached. The sky was covered in gray clouds; they blew quickly across the heavens, changing shape and emptying out as heavy rain.

A wave so high she couldn't see the top of it reared up in front of her. She tried to scream but no sound came from her mouth. She tried again. Her throat felt ready to burst. She put her hand to her mouth to see why the sound wasn't coming, but it wasn't her mouth she felt. It was something so soft and so odd that she couldn't tell what it was. Then she saw her hand and it wasn't her hand; it was a thin stick-like thing as black as night. It was the front leg of a butterfly. Suddenly she could feel the wings growing out of her back. She tried to move them, to lift off and escape the storm.

She began to cry. Suddenly, even while she was still in the storm, as if she could see in two places at the same time, she saw other butterflies. She knew that they were her friends. But they weren't really with her. She could see them but they were somewhere else. There were flowers, lots and lots of flowers, dusty rose colored flowers and beige flowers and lavender flowers. They were everywhere and her friends flitted from one flower to the next, each more beautiful than the last. She felt that they missed her but they didn't know where she was or what to do.

She awoke to the stillness of her own bedroom.

For a long time she lay in the bed remembering what it had felt like to be a butterfly. In the darkness she held her hands in front of her eyes. They were as dark as the surrounding night. As dark as butterfly legs. And she moved her tongue around her lips. As often as she had done this in the past her lips had never felt so strange. Her tongue was dry and her lips felt dry. She wanted to put the light on and look in the mirror at those lips. She didn't, though; she lay silently and thought of the sea rising and falling and of that land where butterflies sipped from the soft cups of flowers.

Black and Orange

At breakfast her mother, on first seeing her, exclaimed, "Ellie, what's wrong, darling?!"

For a second Ellie wondered if her mother was seeing her butterfly lips and she put her hand to her face, only to touch her own small, soft mouth.

"I'm all right," Ellie insisted.

Her father entered the room, stopped, looked at her closely and sat down.

"Good morning," he said.

"Hello." Her voice was low and she was afraid to look at him. She didn't want him saying anything about her.

"She doesn't have a fever," her mother said, "but she looks like something the cat dragged in. Honestly, Ellie, if you're sick, I want to hear it and we'll take you to the doctor's."

"I'm not sick...."

Ellie shook cereal out of the box and poured milk over it. She forced herself to eat.

"You know, you haven't said a thing to us about your Halloween costume," her mother said. "You said you were going to make one. Do you want to tell us what it is?"

Ellie shook her head.

"But, darling, you always show us your

costume."

When Ellie showed no sign of answering, her mother touched her husband's arm as a signal for him to bring up the move.

"Ellie," he said, "do you want to tell us what's wrong?"

"Nothing's wrong. Honestly. I have to go to school now."

And she grabbed her school things and left before her parents could say anything more.

At school Ellie noticed for the first time that the Halloween decorations, which must have been up for two weeks, were mostly in black and orange. Orange pumpkins and black witches and spiders. When she saw them, it was as if someone had stolen the colors from the place where they rightly belonged.

At lunch, she sat in the noisy, crowded cafeteria with her friends but didn't eat and their words floated about her without ever entering her head.

"Ellie, are you listening, girl?" her friend Regina, sitting beside her and bumping her arm, was saying. She put her face near Ellie's. "Hello! I'm talking to you...are you listening?"

Ellie looked at her. "Yes."

Regina raised her voice and spoke slowly, as if talking with a deaf person, "I asked if you wanted me to stop over for you tonight, to go trick or treatin'."

"I don't know...I don't feel so good. Maybe you should go out without me...you know, if I don't show up...."

Regina's eyebrows popped up in an 'oh my, my!' look and Ellie knew that she shouldn't have said what she did.

chapter eight

Halloween

All day Ellie had a light giddiness in her head. It was as if all the butterflies that had gone through Cape May were flying through her. She thought about her dream. And she thought about the real Monarch that she had put into the bay. She saw it as tiny and alone under an enormous sky. Somewhere a forestful of butterflies was waiting for it.

She thought about her costume for that evening. Even now it was sitting in the closet waiting to be filled with life. On the one hand, she couldn't wait to slip it on, to feel just like the lost Monarch, but also there was something scary and terribly sad about it.

During dinner her parents watched her closely. They were so busy watching her that they barely ate their own food.

"I can't eat any more," said Ellie and pushed her plate away.

"Saving room for Halloween candy?" her father asked with a weak laugh.

"I suppose so."

Her mother made a small tsking noise as she removed Ellie's plate, then said, "Do we get to see that costume now?"

Ellie rose from the table and walked to her room. Her heart began to beat fast when one at a time she laid the parts of her costume on the bed. First the black body-suit, as black as deep night. Then the raggedy orange wings, suddenly glowing as if a light were shining on them. And last the small black mask, covering just her eyes so that her nose and mouth could be seen, and a pair of thin black gloves which would match up with her black sleeves so that her thin arms would be black from shoulder to finger tip.

Hurriedly, with nervous fingers, she took off her jeans and blouse. She pulled on the body-suit, straightening out the wrinkles and trying not to think what she was doing.

But as soon as the black cloth touched her skin, she had goose bumps over her entire body. Then she was warm all over. Beads of sweat formed on her upper lip and small drops flowed

slowly down her back. Then she felt the goose
bumps again but there was no coldness attached
to them.

One after the other she put her arms
through the rubber bands that held the wings
to her. The bent flap was there, right by her ear.

When the Monarchs Fly

Quickly she wriggled her fingers into the gloves and with a deliberate move covered her eyes with the mask.

She wanted so badly to look at herself in the mirror but she couldn't stand still. Her feet took quick, small steps around the room, almost like a dance she didn't know she knew. Then her arms began to beat and the wings were like large, delicate fans.

How strangely alive she seemed! Hot, small tears were running down her face from under the mask.

She saw her black hand reach out and turn the handle of the door. Her mother and father were still seated at the kitchen table. She saw the smiles on their faces turn to bewilderment when she didn't stop but, on her toes, she performed her butterfly dance around the room.

"Darling," her mother said, "stand still a

minute so we can look at you."

"Okay, Ellie, slow down...!" her father said.

Instead, she skipped to the front door, opened it and darted into the night. Her mother ran to the door.

"Ellie, come back here! You don't even have your Halloween bag! And don't leave the neighborhood!"

Ellie was down the front walk and never looked back. Her arms moved up and down, her feet stuttered in short, mincing steps, then she raced freely down the street. The orange wings banged against her as if pushing her faster and faster.

Home

The lights in the neighboring houses seemed miles away. Overhead, in the cloudy sky, there was only darkness. Ellie could hear the air being sucked into her lungs through her mouth. But still her tongue reached out to taste the heavy salt air of the nearby sea.

Her feet couldn't stop if she had wanted

them to. Other children out trick or treating in their costumes as ghouls and monsters and pirates saw her and shouted.

"Hey! What are you doing? Are you from this neighborhood?"

In answer, she threw her arms out, spun around and raced past them.

The neighborhood wasn't large and when she was at its boundary, near the bridge to the harbor, she saw some costumed figures trooping from a house, their hands stuffing goodies into their bags. The door was open and a woman stood in the light. Ellie ran up the steps and into the living room. It was Mrs. Greer's house.

"My goodness!" exclaimed Mrs. Greer, "Who is this pretty butterfly?"

Ellie pirouetted. Mrs. Greer's old mother, sitting in her green wing chair in the corner, threw her hands in front of her face at the suddenness of Ellie's entrance. On a table were apples, cookies, a few candy bars and piles with five nickels each. Ellie grabbed an apple, held it to her mouth, then dropped it back. Her eyes took in everything in the room as if tasting it all.

"Where's your bag, girl?" asked Mrs. Greer.

Ellie threw her hands out, almost slapping at Mrs. Greer's hands, and brushed past her.

When she saw children leaving a house, she breathlessly ran in. In this way, she dashed up the walks and into the living rooms of Mrs. Dunlap, Mrs.Evers, Mrs. Crane and Regina's house where old Mr. Fortino said, "Hey! Hey!" She took nothing but spun around in the rooms. It was as if she was entering all the brightly colored flowers of her Cape May neighborhood for the last time.

She saw the door open at Mrs. Howell's house and a parade of children came out. This was the most decorated house in the neighborhood, with sheeted ghosts hanging from the trees and spiders' nests of twine dripping from the eaves. At the top of a flight of six wooden steps her foot hit the porch board and she tripped headlong into the living room.

Mr. Howell, a heavy, bearded man, was in front of the television. Startled, he looked up and frowned as Ellie stumbled around his living room. Mrs. Howell tried to grab her.

"What on earth are you doing?" she said.

In a blur Ellie saw the picture on the wall of the Howells' son, Jim, who was in the army. She saw the stairs leading up, the kitchen behind the dining room.

The room seemed to be spinning. And she spun with it. Then she made a break for the door.

Brushing the door frame, she made it

through but her legs were very wobbly. Small grinning pumpkins lined the short flight of steps and her foot came down hard on one and she smashed it and with a cry she was pitched to the side and fell spinning down the stairs to land with a thud on her head and shoulder. The right wing was crushed beneath her. Her mind was all fuzzy and tried to hold on; she tried to stare at the chrysanthemums in a flower bed in front of her and keep her mind there but it left her like something speeding away.

She awoke to see the concerned faces of Mr. and Mrs. Howell close to hers.

"Ellie, are you all right?" Mrs. Howell was asking.

"I don't want to leave...!" Ellie cried.

Ellie's mask was on her chest. She felt the ground beneath her, damp from the misty sea air.

"Don't you move," Mr. Howell said. "I

phoned for
the rescue squad and they
said for you to stay still."

While her heart
fluttered wildly in her chest,
Ellie forced her eyes closed
and then the rescue squad van pulled up. A
young man in a white uniform asked her to
move her arms and legs. When she did, he asked
her if she felt she could get up. The thought
went through her mind that if she could only

get up she could run away. She tried to push herself up but her arms were as weak as a baby's and she fell back to the ground. Then he carefully put her on a stretcher and, with a young woman, took her to the van.

"Where are you taking me?" there was panic in her voice.

"Just to see if...," the young woman said.

"But I'm all right! I am! Please! Look, I'm all right...." And Ellie pushed herself to sit up, her eyes as wide open as she could make them. "Please, I'm all right...!"

From the front seat the young man looked to the young woman.

She looked closely at Ellie's pleading face, then nodded that there was no need to go to the hospital.

"Okay," he said, "but when we get to your house, you're going inside on that stretcher."

The lights from the rescue squad van flashed blue and red, bringing Ellie's parents to the door.

With the young man at one end and the young woman at the other, Ellie was brought in on the stretcher. She was seated upright, her eyes on the worried faces of her parents. The orange wings were bent and dirty, her black body-suit smeared with dust and wet dirt from her fall.

In a rush, her mother took her in her arms even before Ellie was off the stretcher.

"What happened?! Ellie...!"

"Don't make me leave...."

"Darling...don't cry...nobody's making you leave...."

Her father was with them, his arms wrapped around both of them.

"She heard us, I knew it," he said to his

wife. "Isn't that right, Ellie, you heard us talking about having to move?"

Ellie was crying.

"I don't want to leave...!"

"Nobody wants to leave, Ellie," he said, cradling her head in his hand. "And maybe...maybe nobody has to." He looked to his wife and nodded. "There are worse things than being first mate for a while. Jobs open up...all the time."

"We love it here, too," her mother said.

"And I'll tell you," her father whispered, "if ever the time comes for us to leave, I promise you we'll come back at Monarch time. Every year. Wherever we are. We'll come back, even if we have to put on cardboard wings and fly here."

"Promise?" Ellie asked.

"You bet!"

"Come on, butterfly," her mother said,

"we've been waiting all night for you to come back. Let's go in."

When the Monarchs Fly

About the Monarch Butterfly

Besides being so beautiful, the monarch butterfly has two other qualities that help make it one of the wonders of nature. One is its ability to change — to go from an egg, to a caterpillar, to a pupa and finally to the glory of the full-grown butterfly. The second quality is its power of migration, to fly great distances each year, from as far away as Canada to the Sierra Madre Mountains of Mexico.

The monarch egg is a tiny thing. But after it hatches, about five days after being laid, it is a striped caterpillar and grows quickly. It eats nothing but the milkweed plant leaves on which the egg was set. Within two weeks it has its adult length of about two inches. As its size increases, it sheds its skin five times.

At this time it leaves the milkweed plant and finds a safe place to undergo the tremendous change from a crawling creature to a flying one. The caterpillar hangs by a silky thread and throws off its last skin, under which is a hardening, jade-green shell which will protect it until it emerges a day later. Hemolymph, the life-fluid of insects, flows from its stomach, filling out the wings and body, bringing the butterfly to its adult size. It no longer eats like a caterpillar but, with a tongue like a straw, sips nectar from flowers.

In late summer and early autumn the monarchs begin their long flight southward. Driven by instinct, they crowd the sky with their brilliant colors. There are two pathways the monarchs take, one east of the continental divide and the other to the west of it. They spend the winter in large protected areas called roosts, though even here there is concern about loss of habitat through logging and land development. When warm weather returns in the north, so do the monarchs, bringing light and joy to all who see them.

About the Author

Robert J. Myers has a house in Cape May, New Jersey, where monarchs stop to admire the flowers and ask directions to Central America.

About the Artist

Cricket McGehee is a painter who resides in Harvey Cedars, New Jersey. She has been know to rescue stunned Monarchs along the road while walking her dog.

Down The Shore Publishing offers other book and
calendar titles (with a special emphasis on the mid-Atlantic
coast). For a free catalog, or to be added to our mailing list,
just send us a request:

Down The Shore Publishing
P.O. Box 3100
Harvey Cedars, NJ 08008

www.down-the-shore.com